Munsch at Play

Eight Stage Adaptations for Young Performers

Plays by Irene N. Watts

Original Stories by Robert Munsch

We acknowledge the support of the Canada Council for the Arts, the Ontario Arts Council, and the Government of Canada through the Canada Book Fund (CBF) for our publishing activities.

 ONTARIO ARTS COUNCIL
CONSEIL DES ARTS DE L'ONTARIO

Cataloging in Publication

Watts, Irene N., 1931-
      Munsch at play : eight stage adaptations for young performers : plays / adapted by Irene N. Watts ; original stories by Robert Munsch.

Summary: Angela's airplane — Stephanie's ponytail — Mortimer — 50 below zero — Mud puddle — Millicent and the wind — Murmel, murmel, murmel — The paper bag princess.
ISBN 978-1-55451-230-0 (bound)

      1. Munsch, Robert N., 1945- —Adaptations. I. Title.

PS8595.A873M86 2010   jC812'.54   C2009-905313-6

Distributed in Canada by:

Firefly Books Ltd.
66 Leek Crescent
Richmond Hill, ON
L4B 1H1

Published in the U.S.A. by:

Annick Press (U.S.) Ltd.
Distributed in the U.S.A. by:
Firefly Books (U.S.) Inc.
P.O. Box 1338
Ellicott Station
Buffalo, NY 14205

Printed in China.

Visit us at: www.annickpress.com

For Vicki Duncan and the students of Seaview Community School.
And for Elizabeth Conway, and the students of Gateway Theatre.
—I.N.W.

Contents

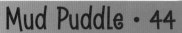

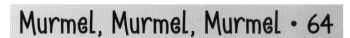

Preface

The following adaptations of some of the most well-loved Robert Munsch stories have been retold and performed in a variety of styles by students of all ages for many years. Children have improvised in groups or as a class, using mime and movement as an alternative to designed set pieces. They have experimented with innovative casting and performed the stories in groups as small as four and larger than twenty!

Groups have used more than one narrator and enjoyed multi-casting.

Performances have taken place indoors and out, on stages, in corridors, classrooms, gymnasiums, and in tents.

These adaptations have challenged students to come up with innovative ideas in every form of presentation, from standard proscenium to theater in the round.

The art of narrative and timing—especially when there is audience participation, the use of sound and silence, many opportunities for arts, crafts, stage design, and costuming, and the use of "found" materials—have enriched the dramatic experience and enhanced class collaboration.

Storytelling through drama, and working together in large groups where everyone has an important role to play, has been as satisfying to the participants as it has to the audience. Performers as young as seven and eight have worked as happily and harmoniously as teenagers, and often in a drama club, as part of a mixed age group.

The following suggestions for casting, staging, set design, props, and costumes are intended as a starting point—one possible way. You and your students will discover many others. Let the power of Robert Munsch's stories and your own creativity be your guide.

Running Time

Each play can be performed in 8 to 10 minutes, but much depends on the space, kinds of participation, costuming, and changes and size of cast. Presentations, if two or three of the stories are put together, can be given in 20 to 30 minutes, allowing for a change-over of cast.

Enjoy!
Irene N. Watts

Angela's Airplane

CAST

- Narrator
- Father
- Angela
- Wings (two)
- Airplane Lights (two)
- Radio Voice
- Airport Personnel: luggage handlers, firefighters, traffic cop, ambulance people, air stewards, travelers, businesspeople, families—variety of ages
- Doctor
- Truck Driver
- Secretary
- Nurse

STAGING

The CAST sits on the floor around the playing area in a half-circle. Their focus is on the NARRATOR and the actors.

Exits and entrances are created by characters entering the playing area and returning to their places when finished.

An exit may be as simple as a character facing upstage away from the audience.

ANGELA and her FATHER are seated next to each other at the start of the play.

SET DESIGN

A barstool, chair, or box for the NARRATOR is set downstage right or left (close to the audience).

A small stepladder for ANGELA, center, with steps facing upstage (away from the audience), represents the airplane.

One bench or two boxes/chairs, is placed on *each* side of the airplane (stepladder).

A hat/coat stand is placed upstage right or left (or hats may be placed on the floor in front of the cast).

PROPS AND COSTUMES

- the button board: large circles, painted or made of felt in red, yellow, black, and green
- two flashlights
- two cutout wings
- hats/caps for FATHER and AIRPORT PERSONNEL

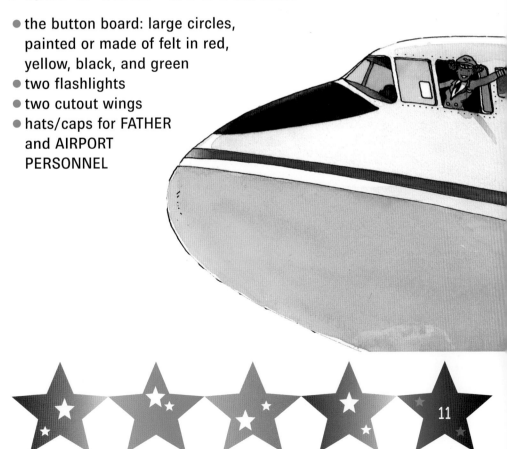

NARRATOR: This story is called *Angela's Airplane*. One day, Angela's father said:

FATHER: I'm taking you to the airport.

(The CAST appears as designated characters in the airport. The two actors playing WINGS sit on either side of the stepladder. The two actors responsible for AIRPLANE LIGHTS sit beside them and help to support the WINGS.)

NARRATOR: They started off looking at stuff together.

(ANGELA is busy examining the scene and does not see her FATHER exit. FATHER returns to his place and removes hat.)

NARRATOR: But then a terrible thing happened … Angela's father got lost.

ANGELA: Where's my dad?

(She looks for him.)

NARRATOR: Angela looked everywhere for her father.

CAST: On top of airplanes, under airplanes, beside airplanes.

ANGELA: I can't find him anyplace.

NARRATOR: Angela decided to look inside an airplane.

ANGELA: I've never been inside an airplane before. I'll try this one.

NARRATOR:	She saw one with an open door and climbed up the steps.
NARRATOR, CAST, ANGELA:	One, two, three, four, right to the top.
ANGELA:	There's no one here at all. I'll just look around and sit right here in the front. What a lot of buttons! *(NARRATOR holds up the button board.)* I *love* pushing buttons. (*To CAST*) Don't you think it would be okay if I pushed just one button?
CAST:	Weeelll …
ANGELA:	Oh yes, it's okay. Yes, yes, yes, yes.
NARRATOR:	Slowly she pressed …
ANGELA:	The bright red button.
NARRATOR, CAST:	Right away, the door closed. *(Doing the action)*
ANGELA:	I'd better push just one more. Don't you think it would be okay if I pushed just one more button?
CAST:	Weeelll …
ANGELA:	Oh yes, it's okay. Yes, yes, yes, yes.
NARRATOR:	Slowly she pressed …
ANGELA:	The yellow button.

AIRPLANE LIGHTS:	Right away, the lights came on. *(They switch on flashlights.)*
ANGELA:	I'd better push just one more button. Don't you think it would be okay if I pushed just one more button?
CAST:	Weeelll …
ANGELA:	Oh yes, it's okay. Yes, yes, yes, yes.
NARRATOR:	Slowly she pressed …
ANGELA:	The green button.
NARRATOR, WINGS:	Right away, the motor came on.
CAST:	VROOM, VROOM, VROOM, VROOM.
NARRATOR, WINGS:	And the plane started to move.
	(ANGELA starts to vibrate in her seat. WINGS move slowly up and down.)
ANGELA:	Yikes, what'll I do now?
NARRATOR:	So Angela pushed all the buttons, and …
NARRATOR, CAST:	The airplane took off and went right up in the sky.
	(WINGS stand.)
ANGELA:	This is very high up. I don't know how to get down. I'm gonna get killed.
NARRATOR:	There was one button left—the black button.

ANGELA: I'll just push this one.

NARRATOR: It was the RADIO button and a voice said …

RADIO VOICE: Bring back that airplane, you thief, you.

ANGELA: I am not a thief. My name is Angela, I'm five years old, and I don't know how to fly airplanes.

RADIO VOICE: Oh, dear. Well, listen carefully, Angela. Take the steering wheel and turn it to the left.

ANGELA: Left?

(CAST raises their left hands.)

ANGELA: Oh, left.

NARRATOR: Very slowly, the airplane went in a big circle.

(WINGS circle the stage once in unison.)

RADIO VOICE: Okay, now pull back on the wheel.

ANGELA: Pull back. *(With great effort)*

NARRATOR, CAST: Slowly, the airplane returned to the runway.

(WINGS sit and do actions.)

NARRATOR, CAST: It hit once and bounced. It hit and bounced again. It hit and one wing scraped the ground.

(CAST makes sounds.)

NARRATOR, CAST:	Right away, the whole plane smashed and broke into little pieces.
	(*WINGS return to original places among the CAST. ANGELA sits on the ground.*)
NARRATOR:	At last, Angela got up.
	(*ANGELA rises and examines herself carefully. AIRPORT PERSONNEL and FATHER put on appropriate hats.*)
ANGELA:	Good, not a scratch anywhere.
NARRATOR:	Cars, trucks, and ambulances came speeding toward Angela. And right in front was Angela's father.
FATHER:	Angela, are you all right?
ANGELA:	Yes.
FATHER:	Oh, Angela, I'm so glad (*hugs her*), but the plane isn't all right.
ANGELA:	I know. It's in little pieces. It was a mistake. I was looking for you.
FATHER:	Well, Angela, promise me you'll never fly another plane.
ANGELA:	I promise.
FATHER:	Are you sure?

ANGELA: I promise, I promise, I promise.
            (They freeze.)

NARRATOR: Angela didn't fly an airplane again for a
            very long time. But when she grew up …

            (She steps out of the freeze.)

ANGELA: I didn't become a doctor.

            *(Actors in appropriate tableaux for each
            career mentioned)*

ANGELA: I didn't become a truck driver.
            I didn't become a secretary.
            I didn't become a nurse.
            I became an airplane pilot.

            *(ANGELA goes up the steps again. WINGS
            return to seats beside stepladder.)*

NARRATOR: So Angela couldn't keep her promise.

            (CAST bows.)

Stephanie's Ponytail

CAST

- Narrator
- Mother
- Stephanie
- Teacher
- Principal
- Class of students (any number)

STAGING

This is an ideal play to involve the entire class. The students sit around the playing area in a horseshoe (U shape), participating as audience/actors.

SET DESIGN

This play is enhanced by having little or no set. The locations of home and school are obvious to the audience by the presence of MOTHER at home and STUDENTS at school.

A chair, box, or barstool for the NARRATOR is placed downstage left or right.

A room divider—a movable bookshelf or a rolling blackboard— placed upstage, center, helps quick exits and entrances from home to school.

PROPS AND COSTUMES

Actors need to be responsible for their personal props!

- Costumes, with the exception of the TEACHER, PRINCIPAL, and MOTHER (who might want to add an appropriate costume piece or glasses), are regular daily wear.
- A hair elastic or scrunchie is required for each student.
- Students also need their own hairbrush or comb to keep in their pockets or in a purse, for quick access.
- a mirror
- one pair of panty hose, cut down for each student, to simulate baldness
- a flash card with the word **BOYS**

NARRATOR:	This is the story of *Stephanie's Ponytail*.
	(*STEPHANIE and MOTHER enter and stand center. MOTHER holds up a mirror, and STEPHANIE tries out some hairstyles.*)
NARRATOR:	One day, Stephanie said to her mom:
STEPHANIE:	None of the kids in my class have a pony-tail. I want a nice ponytail coming right out the back.
MOTHER:	I can do that. Hold still and I'll give you a nice ponytail, coming right out the back.
	(*She gives STEPHANIE the mirror to hold. When she sees her ponytail, STEPHANIE is pleased. MOTHER takes back the mirror and exits upstage. STEPHANIE skips once around the stage on her way to school.*)
NARRATOR:	When Stephanie went to school, the other kids looked at her and said:
	(*STUDENTS get up and walk around STEPHANIE, pointing and laughing.*)
STUDENTS:	Ugly, ugly, *very* ugly. (*A bit of improvised dialogue if desired.*)
STEPHANIE:	It's *my ponytail* and *I* like it.
	(*TEACHER enters, claps hands. GIRL STUDENTS freeze in pairs. TEACHER and STEPHANIE exit. STUDENTS do each other's hair up in ponytails. BOYS refuse to join in and return to their places.*)

NARRATOR: The next morning, when Stephanie went to school …

(*Repeat skipping to school. GIRLS parade in front of STEPHANIE, showing off.*)

NARRATOR: The other girls had ponytails coming out the back.

STEPHANIE: You are all a bunch of copycats. You do just whatever I do. You don't have a brain in your heads!

(*STEPHANIE exits and GIRL STUDENTS return to their places. MOTHER enters, holding the mirror.*)

MOTHER: Stephanie, would you like a ponytail coming out the back, this morning?

STEPHANIE: No.

MOTHER: No? Then that's that. That is the only place you can do ponytails.

STEPHANIE: No, it's not. I want one coming out the side, just above my ear.

MOTHER: Very strange … are you sure that is what you want?

STEPHANIE: Yes.

(*MOTHER hands over the mirror and proceeds.*)

NARRATOR:	When the ponytail was done, Stephanie said:
STEPHANIE:	I like it.
	(*She returns the mirror to her MOTHER, who exits. STEPHANIE goes skipping off to school as before.*)
NARRATOR:	When she went to school, the other kids saw her and said:
	(*They circle STEPHANIE, pointing and laughing.*)
STUDENTS:	Ugly, ugly, *very* ugly.
STEPHANIE:	It's *my ponytail* and *I* like it.
	(*TEACHER enters, claps hands, all freeze including four of the BOYS, and STEPHANIE runs back home while STUDENTS make ponytails.*)
NARRATOR:	Next morning when Stephanie came to school, all the girls and even some of the boys had nice ponytails coming out right above their ears.
STEPHANIE:	Copycats!
	(*She runs home. STUDENTS return to their places.*)

MOTHER:	Stephanie, would you like a ponytail coming out the back this morning?
STEPHANIE:	NNNO!
MOTHER:	No? Would you like one coming out the side?
STEPHANIE:	NNNO!
MOTHER:	No? Then that's that, there is no other place you can do ponytails.
STEPHANIE:	Yes there is. I want a ponytail coming out the top of my head like a tree.
NARRATOR:	Very strange!
MOTHER:	That's very, very strange. Are you sure that is what you want?
STEPHANIE:	Yes, I'm sure.
NARRATOR:	So her mom gave Stephanie a nice ponytail coming out of the top of her head like a tree. When Stephanie went to school, the other kids saw her and YOU know what they said:
STUDENTS:	Ugly, ugly, *very* ugly.
STEPHANIE:	It's *my ponytail* and *I* like it.
	(*TEACHER enters, claps her hands, CAST freezes and makes new ponytails. STEPHANIE runs home.*)

NARRATOR: Next day all of the girls and *all* of the boys had ponytails coming out the top of their heads. Stephanie said:

STEPHANIE: You look like you've got broccoli growing out of your heads. COPYCATS!

(STEPHANIE runs back home, STUDENTS return to their places.)

MOTHER: Stephanie, would you like a ponytail coming out the back this morning?

STEPHANIE: NNNO!

MOTHER: No? Would you like one coming out the side?

STEPHANIE: NNNO!

MOTHER: No? Would you like one coming out at the top?

STEPHANIE: NNNO!

MOTHER: Then that is definitely that. There is no other place you can do ponytails.

STEPHANIE: Yes, there is. I want one coming out the front and hanging down in front of my nose!

MOTHER: But nobody will know if you are coming or going. Are you sure that is what you want?

STEPHANIE: Yes, I'm sure.

NARRATOR:	So her mom gave Stephanie a nice ponytail coming out the front.
MOTHER:	Be careful, Stephanie.
STEPHANIE:	I will.
	(*STEPHANIE skips off to school, and STUDENTS—as trees, cars, houses, and the PRINCIPAL—position themselves in frozen tableaux for STEPHANIE to bump into.*)
NARRATOR:	But on the way to school, she bumped into four trees, three cars, two houses, and one Principal.
	(*After each bump, CAST and STEPHANIE make appropriate sound effects.*)
PRINCIPAL:	Look where you are going, Stephanie!
STEPHANIE:	Yes sir, sorry.
	(*STEPHANIE checks herself for scrapes while CAST returns to the classroom and lines up in order of height across the stage.*)
NARRATOR:	When she finally got to her class, the other kids said …
STUDENTS:	Ugly, ugly, *very* ugly.
STEPHANIE:	It's *my ponytail* and *I* like it.
	(*STEPHANIE runs back home, and all the STUDENTS pair up to create new ponytails.*)

NARRATOR:	The next day all the girls and boys had ponytails hanging down in front of their noses. They bumped into desks …
CAST:	Whoops.
NARRATOR:	They bumped into each other …
CAST:	Sorry!
NARRATOR:	They bumped into walls …
CAST:	Ouch!
NARRATOR:	And by mistake, THREE girls went into …
	(*NARRATOR holds up a card: BOYS. Three GIRLS turn upstage as if to exit.*)
BOYS:	Get out of our WASHROOM!
GIRLS:	(*Scream, return to places.*)
NARRATOR:	When Stephanie got to school the next day, she yelled:
STEPHANIE:	You are a bunch of brainless copycats. Just you wait until tomorrow. I'm going to have … shaved my head.
	(*STEPHANIE goes home, MOTHER greets her. STEPHANIE whispers in her MOTHER'S ear; they exit. Students sit facing upstage, away from the audience, to put on their panty hose.*)

27

NARRATOR: Next morning, the teacher came in. She had shaved her head, and she was … bald.

(TEACHER enters.)

NARRATOR: Next came the boys. They had shaved their heads, and they were … bald.

(BOYS enter and line up.)

NARRATOR: When the girls came in, they had shaved their heads, and they were … bald too!

(GIRLS line up. STEPHANIE skips to school.)

NARATOR: The last person to come to school was Stephanie.

STEPHANIE: I decided to have a ponytail coming right out the back!

(CAST bows.)

Mortimer

CAST

- Narrator
- Mother
- Mortimer
- Father
- 17 Brothers and Sisters
- 2 Police Officers

STAGING

The playing space is divided into two by a set of short steps of two—three risers, each smaller than the one below. Or the stairs may be mimed. Stage right is MORTIMER's bedroom. Stage left represents downstairs.

The NARRATOR is close to the audience, on a box/chair stage right.

MOTHER and MORTIMER stand center, at the start of the story.

Other ACTORS are downstairs. FATHER is in a chair, center left. The BROTHERS and SISTERS sit upstage.

The POLICE OFFICERS sit in the front row, among the audience, with their hats placed in front of them.

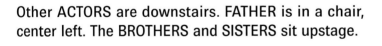

SET DESIGN

- a bed (rollaway cot, bench, boxes, or chairs)
- FATHER's chair
- steps (risers) pushed together in different directions facing away from each other

PROPS AND COSTUMES

- MORTIMER in pajamas or shorts and T-shirt
- newspaper for FATHER
- police hats
- blanket and pillow for MORTIMER's bed

NARRATOR:	This is the story of Mortimer, who liked to make noise. Every night, Mortimer's mother took him upstairs, threw him into bed, and said:
MOTHER:	Mortimer, be quiet.

(MORTIMER nods yes and pulls the blanket over his head.)

NARRATOR:	But …
CAST:	Thump, thump, thump, thump, thump.
NARRATOR:	As soon as his mother got to the bottom of the stairs …

(MORTIMER sits up and sings.)

MORTIMER:	Clang, clang, rattle-bing-bang. Gonna make my noise all day. Clang, clang, rattle-bing-bang. Gonna make my noise all day.

(FATHER throws down newspaper.)

NARRATOR:	Mortimer's father heard that noise and came upstairs.
CAST:	Thump, thump, thump, thump, thump.
NARRATOR:	He opened the door and yelled:

FATHER:	Mortimer, be quiet.
	(MORTIMER nods yes and pulls the blanket over his head.)
NARRATOR:	But ...
CAST:	Thump, thump, thump, thump, thump.
NARRATOR:	As soon as his father got to the bottom of the stairs ...
	(MORTIMER sits up and sings.)
MORTIMER:	Clang, clang, rattle-bing-bang. Gonna make my noise all day. Clang, clang, rattle-bing-bang. Gonna make my noise all day.
NARRATOR:	When Mortimer's 17 brothers and sisters heard that noise ...
CAST:	Thump, thump, thump, thump, thump.
NARRATOR:	They yelled in a tremendous, loud voice:
BROTHERS, SISTERS:	Mortimer, be quiet!
	(MORTIMER covers his ears and nods yes.)
NARRATOR:	But ...
CAST:	Thump, thump, thump, thump, thump.
NARRATOR:	When they got to the bottom of the stairs ... YOU know what happened next.

(MORTIMER sits up and sings.)

MORTIMER:

Clang, clang, rattle-bing-bang.
Gonna make my noise all day.
Clang, clang, rattle-bing-bang.
Gonna make my noise all day.

NARRATOR:

Everyone got so upset, they called the police.

(ACTORS put on police hats, enter, and listen.)

NARRATOR:

Two police officers came and slowly walked up the stairs ...

CAST:

Thump, thump, thump, thump, thump.

NARRATOR:

They opened the door and in deep police officer voices said:

POLICE OFFICERS:

Mortimer, be quiet.

(MORTIMER pulls the blanket over his head and nods yes.)

NARRATOR:

The police officers walked back down the stairs, but ...

CAST:

Thump, thump, thump, thump, thump.

NARRATOR:

As soon as they got to the bottom of the stairs ...

(MORTIMER sits up and sings.)

MORTIMER: Clang, clang, rattle-bing-bang.
Gonna make my noise all day.
Clang, clang, rattle-bing-bang.
Gonna make my noise all day.

NARRATOR: Well, everyone was so upset they got into a big fight.

(The FATHER gets into a fight with the BROTHERS and SISTERS.)

FATHER: You should set him a better example …

BROTHERS, SISTERS: You spoil him. It's not our fault.

MOTHER: *(To POLICE OFFICERS)* Mortimer's a good boy, except at bedtime.

POLICE OFFICERS: *Shh Shh*, listen.

(CAST freezes, listening.)

NARRATOR: Mortimer got so tired of waiting for some-one to come upstairs, he fell asleep.

(MORTIMER snores three times. Quiet.)
(MORTIMER joins CAST. Bow.)

50 Below Zero

CAST

- Narrator
- Jason
- Father
- Mother
- Sound Effects and Props People (a group of four to six actors)

STAGING

At the start of the play, the NARRATOR and JASON are onstage.

The SOUND and PROPS PEOPLE are seated on the floor and are close to the NARRATOR.

Make sure that a space is left (marked out on the floor) to denote OUTSIDE.

SET DESIGN

- JASON's bed may be as simple as a pillow and coverlet.
- a refrigerator: two **sturdy** boxes stacked on top of each other, or a toy one
- a coat rack for outdoor clothes (Or the PROPS PEOPLE may hand these to JASON as required.)

PROPS AND COSTUMES

- a plastic bath or wash tub
- snowsuits, parkas, socks, and mukluks
- a robe for MOTHER
- pajamas for JASON and his FATHER

NARRATOR:	This story is called *50 Below Zero*. In the middle of the night, Jason was asleep.
	(FATHER enters, climbs on refrigerator, sleeps.)
FATHER: S. EFFECTS:	ZZZZZ ZZZZZ ZZZZZ
NARRATOR:	Then Jason woke up.
	(JASON sits bolt upright.)
JASON:	What's that? What's that? What's that sound?
	(He gets up and mimes opening the kitchen door.)
JASON:	I'll just peek into the kitchen.
NARRATOR:	Jason's father walked in his sleep, and that's why he was sleeping on top of the refrigerator.
JASON:	Oh no. Papa, wake up.
	(JASON'S FATHER jumps down, runs around the kitchen three times, and exits.)
JASON:	This house is going crazy.
	(Yawns and returns to bed)
NARRATOR:	Jason went back to sleep.

JASON: S. EFFECTS:	*ZZZZZ ZZZZZ ZZZZZ*

(During the snoring, two PROPS PEOPLE place the tub in the place designated as bathroom and return to their places.)

NARRATOR:	Then Jason woke up.

(FATHER climbs into the tub. Snores.)

FATHER: S. EFFECTS:	*ZZZZZ ZZZZZ ZZZZZ*
JASON:	What's that? What's that? What's that sound?

(JASON gets up and opens the kitchen door.)

JASON:	No one here. I'd better look in the bathroom. Oh no, he's sleeping in the tub. Papa, wake up!

(FATHER jumps out of tub, runs around three times, and exits.)

NARRATOR:	Jason said ...
JASON:	This house is going *(big yawns)* crazy.
NARRATOR:	Jason went back to sleep.
JASON: S. EFFECTS:	*ZZZZZ ZZZZZ ZZZZZ*

(FATHER enters and comes downstage to where props people placed the cutout tree during the above action.)

NARRATOR: Then Jason woke up.

JASON: What's that? What's that? What's that sound?

(He looks in the kitchen.)

JASON: No one there.

(He looks in the bathroom.)

JASON: No one there.

NARRATOR: But the front door was open, and there were his father's footprints in the snow and ...

JASON: Oh no! It's 50 below zero! My father is outside in just his pajamas. He will freeze like an ice cube. I'd better get dressed and find him!

(PROPS PEOPLE bring coat rack/clothes to JASON.)

S. EFFECTS: Snowsuits, parkas, mittens, socks, and mukluks. Better get dressed!

JASON: And now I'll just follow my papa's footprints.

NARRATOR: He walked and walked until he found his father leaning against a tree.

JASON:	Oh no! Papa, wake up. *(Louder)* Papa, wake up!
	(FATHER is motionless. JASON tries to lift him.)
NARRATOR:	Jason's father was too heavy to pick up. So Jason ran home very fast, got his sled, and pulled him back home.
	(PROPS PEOPLE may help, if required.)
S. EFFECTS:	BUMP, BUMP, BUMP, BUMP.
NARRATOR:	Jason pulled him into the bathroom.
S. EFFECTS:	SCRITCH, SCRITCH, SCRITCH, SCRITCH.
NARRATOR:	He turned on the warm water.
S.EFFECTS:	GLUG, GLUG, GLUG, GLUG.
NARRATOR:	Until the tub was full. Then …
	(FATHER runs around three times and exits.)
JASON:	This house *(yawns)* is going crazy. I have to do something.
NARRATOR:	He got a long rope and tied it to his father's toe. *(Offstage)*
NARRATOR:	Jason went back to sleep.

JASON S. EFFECTS:	ZZZZZ ZZZZZ ZZZZZ
	(FATHER enters, moves center, and freezes, leg in the air, rope tied to his toe.)
NARRATOR:	Then Jason woke up.
JASON:	What's that? What's that? What's that sound?
	(JASON opens the kitchen door.)
JASON:	Good. That's the end of Papa's sleepwalking. Now I can go to sleep.
	(JASON climbs onto the refrigerator.)
NARRATOR:	But in the middle of the night ...
S. EFFECTS:	ZZZZZ ZZZZZ ZZZZZ
NARRATOR:	Jason's mother woke up.
	(MOTHER enters.)
MOTHER:	What's that? What's that? What's that sound?
	(MOTHER mimes opening the kitchen door. All freeze, CAST bows.)

Mud Puddle

CAST

- Narrator
- Jule Ann
- Mother
- Mud Puddle

STAGING

At the opening of the play, JULE ANN and the NARRATOR are onstage at center right and center.

MUD PUDDLE is concealed behind the apple tree and MOTHER is offstage.

SET DESIGN

A rolling board, chalkboard, or screen is up center. It is decorated to look like the front of a house. A set of steps face upstage.

A cutout of an apple tree covers the front of the steps, to hide MUD PUDDLE.

- the sandbox—any box
- a plastic bath or tub
- a coat or hat stand for JULE ANN'S clothes
- a painted box or cutout to represent the doghouse
- a chair, box, or stool for the NARRATOR
- a cutout of a piece of fence

PROPS AND COSTUMES

- a skipping rope
- a wagon to hold JULE ANN'S props
- an oversized shirt for MUD PUDDLE, with strips of mud-colored cloths tied or pinned, to facilitate the "flicking of mud"
- two pieces of yellow foam cut in the shape of bars of soap
- a yellow hooded raincoat
- a front-buttoned T-shirt that JULE ANN can wear over her basic outfit of jeans and T-shirt
- a washcloth

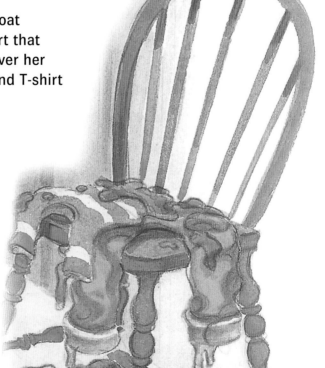

NARRATOR:	This story is called *Mud Puddle*. It was a nice day, and Jule Ann's mother had bought her clean, new clothes.
JULE ANN:	I've got clean, new pants and a clean, new shirt, so I'm going to play under the apple tree. I'm going to skip all the way from here to the apple tree. *(She skips rope, counting each time she completes one turn successfully.)*
NARRATOR:	Unfortunately …
MUD PUDDLE:	Grouch.
NARRATOR:	There was a-a-a-a- *(MUD PUDDLE's head appears.)*
NARRATOR:	Mud Puddle hiding up in the apple tree, and when it saw Jule Ann, it jumped right on her head.
MUD PUDDLE:	I was waiting for you. I love clean clothes.
JULE ANN:	Stop, splutter, aaachoo. *(JULE ANN pushes MUD PUDDLE away. ACTOR moves to his next hiding place.)*
JULE ANN:	Mommy, Mommy, a mud puddle jumped on me and got me muddy all over, even my ears.

MOTHER: Then I'll just have to drop you in the tub and scrub you.

NARRATOR: Her mother scrubbed Jule Ann until she was red all over.

(*JULE ANN yells. There are different sounds for each washing effect.*)

MOTHER: I'll wash out your ears.

JULE ANN: Ow, ah yow.

MOTHER: I'll wash out your eyes.

JULE ANN: (*Repeats screams.*)

MOTHER: I'll wash out your mouth with this wash-cloth.

(*JULE ANN screams with a washcloth in her mouth.*)

NARRATOR: At last, Jule Ann was clean all over.

MOTHER: That's better. (*Kisses the top of her head.*) Now, put on this clean, new shirt and these clean, new pants. And zip them up. All done, now go play. (*MOTHER exits.*)

NARRATOR: Jule Ann looked carefully from left to right.

JULE ANN: I don't see a mud puddle anywhere, so I'm going to play in my sandbox.

NARRATOR: Unfortunately …

MUD PUDDLE:	Grouch.
NARRATOR:	Hiding behind the roof of her house ...
NARRATOR:	There was a-a-a-a-

(MUD PUDDLE's head appears.)

NARRATOR:	Mud Puddle. And when it saw Jule Ann, it jumped right on her head.
MUD PUDDLE:	I was waiting for you. I love clean clothes.
JULE ANN:	Stop, splutter, aaachoo.

(The MUD PUDDLE swirls over and around JULE ANN. She pushes MUD PUDDLE away. MUD PUDDLE moves to his next hiding place.)

JULE ANN:	Mommy, Mommy, a mud puddle jumped on me and got me muddy all over, even my nose.
MOTHER:	Then I'll just have to drop you in the tub and scrub you all over again.

(Repeat previous procedure.)

MOTHER:	I'll wash out your ears.
JULE ANN:	Ow, ah, yow.
MOTHER:	I'll wash out your eyes.
JULE ANN:	*(Repeats screams.)*

MOTHER:	I'll wash out your mouth with this wash-cloth.
	(JULE ANN screams with washcloth in her mouth.)
MOTHER:	I'll wash out your nose.
JULE ANN:	*(Screams.)*
MOTHER:	And I'll wash out your belly button.
JULE ANN:	*(Giggles.)*
NARRATOR:	And, at last, Jule Ann was clean all over.
MOTHER:	That's better. *(Kisses the top of JULE ANN's head.)* All done. Now, put on this clean, new shirt and these clean, new pants and zip them up. Now go play. *(MOTHER exits.)*
NARRATOR:	Suddenly, Jule Ann thought of something …
JULE ANN:	I've got an idea. I'm gonna get my big yel-low raincoat and pull up the hood.
NARRATOR:	She marched into the middle of the yard, but she could not see the mud puddle any-where.
JULE ANN:	I'm gonna call it. Hey! Mud Puddle!!
NARRATOR:	Nothing happened.

JULE ANN:	I'm gonna call it even louder. Hey! Mud Puddle!!
NARRATOR:	Nothing happened.
JULE ANN:	I'm too hot. I think I'll pull back the hood. Do you think that's okay? *(Audience may respond. JULE ANN does so anyway.)*
NARRATOR:	Still, nothing happened.
JULE ANN:	I'm too hot. I'm gonna take off my coat. Do you think it's okay if I take off my coat? *(She does so.)*
NARRATOR:	Unfortunately …
MUD PUDDLE:	Grouch.
NARRATOR:	There was a-a-a-a- *(MUD PUDDLE's head appears.)*
NARRATOR:	Mud Puddle hiding behind the doghouse, and when it saw Jule Ann it jumped right on her head.
MUD PUDDLE:	I was waiting for you. I love clean clothes. *(MUD PUDDLE swirls over and around JULE ANN.)*
JULE ANN:	Stop, splutter, aaachoo.

(MUD PUDDLE moves to the next hiding place.)

JULE ANN: Mommy, Mommy, a mud puddle jumped on me and got me muddy all over, even in my belly button.

MOTHER: Then I'll just have to drop you in the tub and scrub you all over again.

(She scrubs JULE ANN all over.)

MOTHER: I'll wash out your ears.

JULE ANN: Ow, ah, yow!

MOTHER: I'll wash out your eyes.

JULE ANN: No! No! No!

MOTHER: And I'll wash out your mouth.

JULE ANN: *(Screams with washcloth in her mouth.)*

MOTHER: And I'll wash out your nose.

JULE ANN: *(More loud screams)*

MOTHER: And I'll wash out your belly button.

JULE ANN: *(Giggles.)*

NARRATOR: And at last, Jule Ann was clean all over.

MOTHER:	That's better. *(Kisses the top of JULE ANN's head.)* Now, put on a clean, new shirt and button it up the front. And clean, new pants and zip them up. All done, now go play, and try to keep clean. *(MOTHER exits.)*
NARRATOR:	But Jule Ann sat beside the door.
JULE ANN:	I'm afraid to go play, in case that mud puddle jumps out at me.
NARRATOR:	Then, suddenly …
JULE ANN:	I've got an idea.
NARRATOR:	She got a really big, smelly bar of soap and smelled it.
JULE ANN:	Yecch. I'll put it in my pocket.
NARRATOR:	She took another bar of smelly soap and smelled it.
JULE ANN:	Yecch. I'll put that in my other pocket.
NARRATOR:	Then she ran into the middle of the yard and yelled:
JULE ANN:	Hey, Mud Puddle!
NARRATOR:	Mud Puddle jumped right from behind the fence and ran toward Jule Ann.
MUD PUDDLE:	Grouch. I love clean clothes!

NARRATOR:	Jule Ann threw the soap right at Mud Puddle's middle, and Mud Puddle stopped. Then she threw the other one at Mud Puddle, and Mud Puddle said:
MUD PUDDLE:	Awk, yecch, wackh!

(JULE ANN grabs a container of bubble mixture from her wagon and blows soap bubbles. MOTHER enters and does the same.)

NARRATOR:	And Mud Puddle jumped back over the fence, and ran and ran, and never came back because mud puddles hate soap!

(CAST chases MUD PUDDLE once around the stage. Bows.)

Millicent and The Wind

CAST

- Narrator
- Wind
- Millicent
- Mother
- Boy (with red hair, if possible)
- Friend
- Sound Effects (made by four to six actors)
- Village Children (any number)

STAGING

The audience is seated on either side of an aisle, wide enough to allow the WIND, MOTHER, and MILLICENT to walk through.

The VILLAGE CHILDREN are seated on either side of the stage.

SOUND EFFECTS are grouped upstage left or right, diagonally from the NARRATOR, who is seated on a box (PAINTED LIKE A ROCK) downstage.

Triangles, wind chimes, and homemade instruments can be strung across a pole and sounded when the WIND enters from his place at the back of the audience.

MOTHER is offstage.

MILLICENT stands in front of the screen at the start of the play.

SET DESIGN

A screen or rolling blackboard is decorated with trees, clouds, sunshine, and mountains. These could be painted as a mural or made from pieces of cutout felt or origami paper. Large cutouts might also be considered.

PROPS AND COSTUMES

- The WIND wears a loose-fitting garment that allows freedom of movement. Strips of ribbon are tied around his wrists to suggest and help the flow and ripple of the WIND moving at all times.
- a knapsack
- musical instruments (See above suggestions.)

NARRATOR:	This story is about Millicent and the wind. Whisper your names quietly. *(S. EFFECTS whisper, to guide audience.)* That is the way the wind sounded to Millicent one quiet morning.
	(MILLICENT moves center stage.)
NARRATOR:	Millicent lives up here on the mountain with her mother. Millicent can see rocks and trees and sunshine and clouds. She can look at the world. But she has no one to play with—no friends—because it takes three whole days to walk down the mountain to the valley where other children live.
MILLICENT:	I wish I had someone to play with.
	(The WIND sweeps up the aisle.)
WIND:	Hey, Millicent.
S. EFFECTS:	Hey, Millicent. *(Softer echo effect)*
	(During the following exchange, the WIND moves around MILLICENT. S. EFFECTS make gentle wind sounds throughout.)
MILLICENT:	Who's that? Who are you?
WIND:	Who, who, who?
S. EFFECTS:	Who, who, who?
MILLICENT:	Who are you? There are only trees and rocks up here, and they can't talk.

WIND:	I am the wind.
	(WIND rustles gently around her, touching her hair. S. EFFECTS)
MILLICENT:	On no, up here the wind just howls and roars and whistles and blows. It doesn't talk.
WIND:	I am the wind of all the world, I do what I want and talk the way I wish. Today, the sun is yellow, and the day is happy and quiet, so I feel like talking instead of howling. Hello, Millicent.
MILLICENT:	Well, I have lots of time but no friends to talk or play with. Can you play tag?
WIND:	Certainly.
NARRATOR:	So they played touch tag, and shadow tag, running among the trees and rocks. *(S. EFFECTS may join in but return to places when the WIND exits.)*
WIND:	I must go now.
MILLICENT:	Come back tomorrow.
WIND:	I will, I will, I will.
	(WIND exits down the aisle and crouches behind the last audience row.)

NARRATOR:	And the wind came back every day to play with Millicent.
	(The tag game may be repeated or omitted.)
NARRATOR:	One day, Millicent's mother said:
	(MOTHER enters, with knapsack.)
MOTHER:	We are going to walk to the village today. We need to buy lots of things.
MILLICENT:	Will it take three whole days?
MOTHER:	Yes, it will.
	(They exit stage left. WIND rushes in up the aisle.)
WIND:	Who, who, who? Where are you, Millicent?
NARRATOR:	The wind had no one to play tag with and went looking for Millicent.
	(The WIND circles the stage, exits through and around the audience, singing the song of the wind.)
WIND: S.EFFECTS:	*I AM THE WIND, THROUGH THE WORLD I'LL GO. I RATTLE AND ROAR AND WHISTLE AND BLOW THROUGH TOWNS AND FIELDS IN EVERY NOOK. IN SCHOOLS AND YARDS I'LL SEARCH AND LOOK, AND WHEN I FIND MY FRIEND WE'LL PLAY GAMES OF TAG THE WHOLE LONG DAY.*
	(MOTHER and MILLICENT enter during the final line. WIND sits at the back of the audience.)

NARRATOR:	At the end of three days, Mother and Millicent come to the valley.
MOTHER:	Here we are, at last.
	(The CHILDREN come downstage and stare at them. The RED-HAIRED BOY steps forward.)
BOY:	Who are you, where do you come from?
MILLICENT:	I'm Millicent. I live up there on the mountaintop. I have no friends except the wind.
BOY:	*(Laughing)* The wind is nobody's friend.
	(He taunts her and encourages the children to do the same.)
BOY:	Millicent, Millicent, lives on the mountaintop. Go home, Millicent, go home, Millicent, go home, Millicent.
NARRATOR:	Then a strange thing happened. The wind blew in and …
	(WIND enters and rushes up the aisle to the stage. S. EFFECTS throughout)
NARRATOR:	Tumbled the boy about like a leaf, here and there, up, down, all over the place, until his clothes were in tatters and his hair a mess!
	(During this sequence, MILLICENT stays beside the NARRATOR. The CHILDREN gradually return to their places, as if blown by

the WIND. The BOY is the last one to be whirled back to his place. The WIND exits left and MOTHER enters right.)

MOTHER: It's time for us to start the walk home.

MILLICENT: *(As they walk)* I wish the kids had stayed to play with me.

MOTHER: I know, but soon we'll be home.

NARRATOR: It took them three whole days to walk back to the mountain.

(MOTHER and MILLICENT walk around the audience, then up the aisle.)

MILLICENT: We're home!

(WIND rushes in to MILLICENT, center. MOTHER sits beside NARRATOR.)

WIND: Welcome back. I looked for you, I wanted to play.

(WIND starts to chase MILLICENT.)

MILLICENT: Wait, I want to tell you something. *(Stops.)* Wind, you blow through the hair of every child in the world. Can you find me some-one to play with?

WIND: Well, who? Boy or girl?

MILLICENT: It doesn't matter, just get me a friend.

S. EFFECTS:	Roar, rumble, whistle, and blow.
	(The WIND exits, looking for a friend.)
NARRATOR:	The wind rushed away, and he bent the trees and whistled and rumbled, looking for a friend for Millicent.
WIND:	Who? You? You?
	(The WIND looks up and down the CHILDREN, and returns with the designated one.)
NARRATOR:	They looked at each other.
MILLICENT: FRIEND:	Let's play.
NARRATOR:	And they did.
	(NARRATOR and WIND join the cast in a game of tag. Freeze and bow.)

Murmel, Murmel, Murmel

CAST

- Narrator
- Robin
- Baby Voice
- Woman with Stroller
- Cast: cats, diaper salespeople, secretaries, messengers
- Old Lady
- Woman in Fancy Clothes
- Pizza Delivery Man

STAGING

The entire CAST is visible, seated on and around the stage or playing area throughout.

Exits and entrances are made by characters entering the playing area from their places, picking up a prop or costume piece, and returning to their places on cue, after replacing their prop.

At the start of the play, the NARRATOR and the BABY (who sits on the floor beside the NARRATOR) are present, as is ROBIN (who kneels above the sandbox).

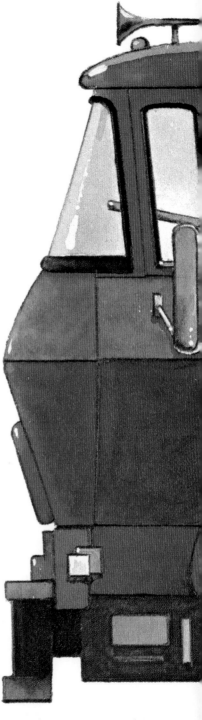

SET DESIGN

- a box or chair for the NARRATOR
- a box (the sandbox) big enough to conceal the baby DOLL at center stage
- a garbage can
- a bench
- a table or rack upstage for props and costume pieces. It may be helpful to have one upstage center, both left and right, behind the CAST to facilitate changes.

PROPS AND COSTUMES

It is suggested that the CAST, because of the variety of characters that they play, assumes only one prop or costume piece for each different character.

- a large baby doll
- a spade
- a baby stroller or buggy, containing a baby doll
- a pizza box
- diaper boxes
- hats, shawls, glasses, and other costume pieces as desired
- notepads, computer cases, cell phone
- newspaper
- cat masks (optional). Cat movements are enough to suggest the felines.

NARRATOR:	This story is called:
CAST:	MMM *(The CAST starts to hum, and the audience is encouraged to do the same. The NARRATOR raises a hand for silence.)*
NARRATOR:	*Murmel, Murmel, Murmel.*
NARRATOR:	When Robin went into her yard to dig in her sandbox, there was a large hole there already. She knelt down beside it and yelled:
ROBIN:	Is anybody down there? *(She listens.)*
ROBIN:	I think I can hear something.
BABY:	Murmel, murmel, murmel.
ROBIN:	Hmm, very strange. *(Loudly)* Is anybody down there?
NARRATOR:	Something said:
BABY:	Murmel, murmel, murmel.
	(ROBIN reaches into the box and pulls out a baby doll.)
ROBIN:	Murmel yourself, I'm only five years old, I can't take care of a baby, but I'll find someone else to take care of you.
NARRATOR:	Robin walked down the street.

(WOMAN pushing a stroller with baby appears.)

ROBIN: Excuse me, do you need a baby?

WOMAN: Heavens, no! I already have a baby.
(WOMAN coos at own baby.)

CAST: You'll need diapers.

NARRATOR: Seventeen diaper salespeople ran after her down the street.

ROBIN: I'll just go on down the street.

(OLD LADY appears.)

ROBIN: Excuse me, do you need a baby?

OLD LADY: Does it pee its pants?

ROBIN: Yes.

OLD LADY: Yecch. Does it have a runny nose?

(ROBIN checks after each question.)

ROBIN: Yes.

OLD LADY: Yecch. Does it dirty its diaper?

ROBIN: Yes.

OLD LADY: Yecch. I already have 17 cats, I don't need a baby.

NARRATOR: Off she went down the street. *(Exit.)*

CAST: *Miauw… (CAST as CATS in sound and movement.)*

NARRATOR: 17 cats jumped out of the garbage can and ran after her.

(Circle stage once and return to places.)

ROBIN: We'll just go on down the street.

(WOMAN IN FANCY CLOTHES appears.)

ROBIN: Excuse me, do you need a baby?

FANCY WOMAN: Heavens, no! I have 17 jobs, lots of money, and no time. I don't need a baby.

CAST: Telephone, miss. Pizza delivery, message waiting, board meeting, conference …

NARRATOR: 17 secretaries, 9 messengers, and a pizza delivery man ran after her.

(They circle the stage twice and return to their places.)

ROBIN: Rats! We'll walk on down the street.

(ROBIN throughout hugs, pats, and is kind to the BABY. A MAN appears, reading a newspaper.)

ROBIN: Excuse me, do you need a baby?

MAN:	I don't know, can it wash my car?
ROBIN:	No.
MAN:	Can I sell it for lots of money?
ROBIN:	No.
MAN:	Well, what's it for?
ROBIN:	It's for loving and hugging and feeding and burping.
MAN:	I certainly don't need that. *(Exit.)*
NARRATOR:	*Nobody* followed him.
	(ROBIN sits down.)
ROBIN:	You are a heavy baby to carry around.
BABY:	Murmel, murmel, murmel.
ROBIN:	Murmel yourself, what am I going to do with you?
NARRATOR:	Suddenly an enormous truck came by and stopped.
	(TRUCK DRIVER leans the cutout truck against the bench and walks around the BABY and ROBIN three times.)
ROBIN:	Do you need a baby?
TRUCK DRIVER:	Weeelll …

BABY:	Murmel, murmel, murmel.
NARRATOR:	The truck driver yelled:
TRUCK DRIVER:	I need you.
NARRATOR:	The truck driver picked up the baby and started walking down the street.
ROBIN:	Wait, you forgot your truck!
TRUCK DRIVER:	I already have 17 trucks, what I need is a baby …
BABY:	Murmel, murmel, murmel.
	(TRUCK DRIVER, BABY, and CAST down center, bow.)

The Paper Bag Princess

CAST

- Narrator
- Princess Elizabeth
- Prince Ronald
- Dragon
- Lady in Waiting 1 and 2
- Forest 1 and 2
- Flames (Two of whom can double as Props People to turn the castle into the cave.)

STAGING

The CAST except for the DRAGON are seated in a semicircle.

At the start of the play, the NARRATOR is downstage right and PRINCESS ELIZABETH is center with PRINCE RONALD. LADY IN WAITING 1 stands beside the NARRATOR, ready to hand the tiara to ELIZABETH on cue.

LADY IN WAITING 2 stands across on stage left beside a clothes rack of "Princess" clothes.

SET DESIGN

A table, upstage center, over which is hung a floor-length cloth or a cutout of the interior of a castle, which may be REVERSED to become the DRAGON'S CAVE. Alternatively, the DRAGON, and later PRINCE RONALD, could be concealed behind a movable bookcase or blackboard, again with appropriate designs for each location. A wheeled cutout, painted differently on both sides, is another option.

- a stool or chair for NARRATOR

PROPS AND COSTUMES

- a DRAGON mask
- a tiara for ELIZABETH
- a princess garment, which is easily removed in the fire, such as a pretty shirt or vest, or short cape
- a paper bag
- branches and twigs to represent the forest
- flame ribbons of red, yellow, and orange
- Actors as fire and forest should have their props in front or behind them for easy access. If fire ribbons are sewn on wrist or arm bands, they are more manageable.

NARRATOR: This story is called *The Paper Bag Princess.* Once upon a time when Elizabeth was a beautiful princess, she lived in a castle …

(LADY IN WAITING 1 hands her a tiara.)

L. IN WAITING 1: And had expensive princess clothes.

(Appropriate cutouts of a castle are wheeled in if needed, also a clothes rack on which several glitzy items are hung. ELIZABETH chooses one.)

NARRATOR: She also had a royal boyfriend.

ELIZABETH: Well, I guess I'll marry Prince Ronald, maybe even next week.

(PRINCE RONALD walks toward her.)

NARRATOR: But unfortunately a dragon …

(Actor puts on dragon mask, emerges, slobbers, grunts, and enters castle, followed by FIRE CAST waving ribbons.)

smashed the castle and burned all of Princess Elizabeth's clothes and carried off Prince Ronald.

DRAGON: Wood, gotcha; clothes, gotcha …

(CAST AS FLAMES wheels off clothes rack and princess cape. LADIES exit.)

PRINCE: Help, help, let go of me.

	(DRAGON exits upstage with PRINCE RONALD, FLAMES return to their places.)
ELIZABETH:	How can I chase the dragon and get back Prince Ronald without my princess clothes?
NARRATOR:	She looked everywhere for something to wear.
ELIZABETH:	All my clothes are burnt up.
L. IN WAITING 2:	Will this do, Your Highness? *(Holds up paper bag.)*
ELIZABETH:	A paper bag? Yes!
NARRATOR:	So she put on the paper bag. It was actually a perfect fit, and she started to follow the messy trail of burned-up forests and horses' teeth left behind by the dragon.
	(CAST AS FOREST 1 creates a path of twisted trees using their bodies and hands.)
ELIZABETH:	I'll chase the dragon and get Ronald back. This forest is scary.
	(NARRATOR and a TREE ACTOR arrange the dragon cave door. FOREST 1 returns to their places.)
NARRATOR:	Suddenly, the trail ended.
ELIZABETH:	This must be the dragon's cave. I'll just knock on the door.

NARRATOR:	The dragon had only just got back from his travels and was pretty sleepy.
	(DRAGON puts out his snout and yawns.)
DRAGON:	*(Roars and sniffs.)* Go away, whatever you are. I love to eat princesses, but I have already eaten a whole castle today. I've been very busy. Come back tomorrow. *(Shuts door.)*
ELIZABETH:	Ow, watch out! You nearly hit my nose.
NARRATOR:	She grabbed the knocker and banged on the door again.
	(Roaring sounds)
DRAGON:	Go away, I'm tired. I love to eat princesses, but I've already eaten one whole castle, one school, two trains, and three police cars today. Come back tomorrow.
ELIZABETH:	*(Shouting)* Wait, I want to ask you something important.
DRAGON:	Well?
ELIZABETH:	Is it true that you are the smartest and fiercest dragon in the whole world?
DRAGON:	Yes, I am.
ELIZABETH:	And is it true that you can burn up 10 forests with your fiery breath?
DRAGON:	Oh yes, anytime! Watch this!

NARRATOR:	Then he took a huge, deep breath.
	(CAST AS FLAMES rises and waves flames. CAST AS FOREST 2 raises twigs, slowly subsides in their places.)
NARRATOR:	And when the dragon breathed out, there was so much fire that he burned up 50 forests.
ELIZABETH:	Fantastic. *(Applauds.)*
NARRATOR:	Then the dragon took another huge breath ...
	(Repeat above FLAMES sequence.)
	And breathed out so much fire that he burned up 100 forests.
ELIZABETH:	Magnificent. *(Applauds. FLAMES return to their places.)*
NARRATOR:	But this time, when the dragon tried to take a huge breath, nothing came out. There wasn't even enough fire left to roast a marshmallow. But Elizabeth is cooking up a plan.
ELIZABETH:	Dragon, is it true that you can fly around the world in just 10 seconds?
DRAGON:	Why yes, anytime. When I say go, you can count the seconds. GO.

NARRATOR:	The dragon jumped up and flew all around the world.
	(DRAGON exits and runs around the audience. NARRATOR and ELIZABETH count.)
NARRATOR:	1 … 10.
	(DRAGON re-enters, gasping.)
DRAGON:	I'm a bit tired, but I did it.
ELIZABETH:	Fantastic. Do it again.
	(DRAGON exits and repeats as above.)
NARRATOR:	So the dragon jumped up and flew around the world. This time it took him 20 seconds. 1 … 20.
DRAGON:	*(Re-enters, gasping)* No more questions. I'm too tired to … talk.
	(Collapses and snores. ELIZABETH tiptoes up to the DRAGON.)
ELIZABETH:	Hey, dragon. Hey, dragon. Hey, dragon.
NARRATOR:	But the dragon was too tired to move. You've done it. Go ahead, open the door.
	(ELIZABETH steps over the dragon and opens the door. PRINCE RONALD enters down center.)

PRINCE:	Elizabeth? Yecch! Boy, are you a mess. You smell like ashes. Your hair is all tangled and you are wearing a dirty, old paper bag. Come back and see me when you're dressed like a real princess.
NARRATOR:	Elizabeth walked all around Prince Ronald, took a huge breath, and said:
ELIZABETH:	Ronald, your clothes are really pretty, and your hair is all neat. You look like a real prince, you smell like a prince, but you are a bum.
PRINCE:	What did you call me?
NARRATOR:	She called you …
ALL:	A bum.
ELIZABETH:	Goodbye, Ronald, you're not the one for me!
NARRATOR:	So they didn't get married after all.

(Freeze. CAST bows.)